Bunnies
in Trouble

Bunnies in Trouble

Susan Hughes

Cover by Susan Gardos
Illustrations by Heather Graham

SCHOLASTIC CANADA LTD.
Toronto New York London Auckland Sydney
Mexico City New Delhi Hong Kong Buenos Aires

Scholastic Canada Ltd.

175 Hillmount Road, Markham, Ontario L6C 1Z7, Canada

Scholastic Inc.

555 Broadway, New York, NY 10012, USA

Scholastic Australia Pty Limited

PO Box 579, Gosford, NSW 2250, Australia

Scholastic New Zealand Limited

Private Bag 94407, Greenmount, Auckland, New Zealand

Scholastic Ltd.

Villiers House, Clarendon Avenue, Leamington Spa,
Warwickshire CV32 5PR, UK

National Library of Canada Cataloguing in Publication

Hughes, Susan, 1960-
    Bunnies in trouble / Susan Hughes ; illustrated by Heather Graham.
(Wild paws ; 3)
ISBN 0-439-98984-1

1. Rabbits–Juvenile fiction. 2. Animal shelters–Juvenile fiction.
I. Graham, Heather, 1959- II. Title. III. Series: Hughes, Susan, 1960- Wild paws ; 3.

PS8565.U42B86 2004   jC813'.54   C2003-905221-4

6 5 4 3 2 1   Printed in Canada   04 05 06 07 08

To Maya and Karen, a dynamic duo.

Thank you to Jody and Dale Gienow of the Muskoka Wildlife Centre for lending their expertise and helpful suggestions to this story.

Contents

Chapter One

Emergency!

"Oh, these are the best Easter posters we've made!" Max exclaimed. Her brown eyes sparkled with delight. "Let's put them on the gate!"

"Good idea," Sarah agreed, her red braids dangling below her hat. "They'll be the first things that visitors to Wild Paws and Claws see when they drive in!"

It was a cold Sunday and the two friends were helping out at the wildlife rehabilitation centre just outside of the town of Maple Hill. They spent several afternoons a week there, and every Saturday they worked as guides, showing visitors around. Sometimes, like today, there was extra work to be done, and so they came on Sundays, too.

Carrying the posters and some tape, Max and Sarah hurried down the stony driveway that led through the parking lot toward the front gate.

"I thought your grandmother was coming this morning," Sarah remarked. She zipped up her spring jacket as they walked.

"Me too," Max said. "She's supposed to be bringing her new friend, Mrs. Peach, to visit Wild Paws. Mrs. Peach has lived in town forever, but she's never come and visited the animals here."

The girls reached the front gate, with its sign that announced: *Wild Paws and Claws Clinic and Rehabilitation Centre*. Below the name was a drawing of a paw print. At the bottom of the gate some green shoots of brave spring plants poked up through last autumn's dead leaves. Max and Sarah taped up the Easter posters below the sign, careful not to step on the shoots.

"Great," said Max, standing back and surveying their work. One poster showed baby animals – ducklings, chicks and bunnies – waddling, scritch-scratching and hopping in a long wobbly line. The other was colourfully decorated with Easter eggs, bunnies and roly-poly puppies. Max had printed *Wild Paws and Claws Welcomes Spring!* on her poster.

"Where should we put up the other Easter posters we made?" Max wondered.

"Let's put them near the animal pens," Sarah said.

The friends headed back up the driveway. Max smiled as she thought about Easter. To her, it meant new wild baby animals being born. It meant spring was on its way. Spring was her favourite time of the year.

They had just reached the parking lot when Grandma's car pulled in. Max was surprised to see three people get out of the car.

"Hello, girls!" Grandma said. "This is my friend, Mrs. Clara Peach. And this is her nephew, Randall."

"Hello there," Mrs. Peach said, giving a little wave of her fingers to Max and Sarah. She had fuzzy white hair and a chubby face. "Nice to meet you both."

The girls greeted the woman. Max looked at Randall. He looked almost as old as a grown-up, but not quite. He had brown eyes, hair that needed cutting and a shirt that wasn't tucked in properly. Max waited for him to say hello, but he was staring off into the distance. He wasn't paying any attention to them.

Mrs. Peach said, "Randall just arrived today,

unexpectedly. He's studying close by at the university, so his mother — my sister — suggested that he come and pay a visit to his dear auntie — me!"

Again, Max waited for Randall to say something. But he didn't. He jammed his hands in his pockets. He glanced at the girls and smiled the tiniest smile, then went back to staring into the distance.

Max looked at Sarah. Sarah rolled her eyes, and Max giggled.

"So, Max," Mrs. Peach cooed. "Why don't you tell me how you are enjoying Maple Hill, now that you've been living here for a while?"

"Oh, I love it!" Max replied. "It's so great to be living in the countryside. Grandma and I get to go on big hikes together. And it's because my family moved here that I met Sarah — and we ended up working at Wild Paws!"

"Why don't you tell Randall how you were introduced to this place?" Mrs. Peach suggested. "You can remind me, too." She lifted her pink collar around her neck as a cool breeze picked up. "And perhaps we could walk toward the animal pens while you explain? I'm getting a touch chilly," she added, patting her curls back into place.

"Good idea," Max said. "They're this way." She

pointed, and she and Sarah began leading the group past the office and toward a path that led through the trees.

"Well, you know that Grandma, my brother David and I found a baby bobcat in the countryside only a few days after we moved to Maple Hill," Max began. The scene flashed back into her mind. She remembered hearing a sad *mew-mew-mew* and searching the rocks at the bottom of the cliff. She remembered her first sight of the tiny creature. Max hadn't known that it was a wild baby bobcat. The animal had looked just like the kitten of a domestic cat – tiny and helpless. Her eyes were closed, and her voice was thin and weak. But when Grandma, Max and David saw the tufts on her ears and her bobbed tail, they realized she was special!

Mrs. Peach nodded, her white curls bouncing. "The bobcat's mother had been killed and you knew the baby wouldn't survive on its own," she said. Then she glanced at her nephew, who was walking beside her along the path. "Randall, listen, dear," she said kindly. "This is right up your alley. Animals."

"I was listening, Aunt Clara," Randall said, in a soft voice.

Max lifted her eyebrows. She was surprised at

Randall's answer. He certainly hadn't seemed to be listening.

Max went on with her story. "So we brought the baby bobcat – who we named Tuffy – here, to Wild Paws and Claws. It's owned by Abbie – Abigail Abernathy. Here at Wild Paws, the idea is to heal any hurt or injured wild animals and then return them to their homes in the woods. But there are some animals that live here permanently. In fact, here's one now."

They had arrived in a clearing in which there was a large circle of pens. Max stopped in front of the first enclosure.

"This is Tippy," she said. The red fox was drinking from his water pan. At the sound of Max's voice, he picked up his head and tilted his ears forward.

"Oh, my," Mrs. Peach exclaimed, putting her hand to her mouth. "He's beautiful. Look at the white fur at the tip of his tail. But the sweet thing only has three legs."

"Right," Max said. "He had an accident when he was a pup. But the main reason he is still here is that he never learned to find his own food. If he were released, he wouldn't be able to survive on his own."

"I see," said Mrs. Peach, with an understanding nod.

Max stole a look at Randall. The young man still didn't seem to be listening to her, but he was no longer staring into the distance. He was gazing intently at Tippy. Randall was absolutely still. His face was calm, and his eyes seemed locked on the red fox.

"Well, it's just so wonderful that this clinic is here for these animals. But wasn't there some problem with Wild Paws staying open?" Mrs. Peach asked.

"Yes." Grandma nodded. "Wild Paws and Claws was in trouble. It had run out of money and was in danger of closing. After we brought Tuffy here, Max and Sarah helped Abbie run an open house to raise money for the clinic."

"Wild Paws is doing pretty well these days," Max added. Then her grin turned into a frown. "But there's still one problem that we haven't solved yet. We don't have a wild-animal vet anymore. The vet who used to volunteer here has retired."

"Oh, but that can't be a problem. Not now anyway," Mrs. Peach said. She clapped her hands together and beamed at Max. Then she turned and looked at her nephew.

Randall didn't say anything. He hadn't taken his eyes off the red fox. Perhaps he hadn't heard what his aunt had said.

Then he spoke in a soft voice. "Perhaps I could help," he said. Randall wasn't looking at Max or at his aunt. He was still gazing at Tippy. It was almost as if he were speaking to him.

Max was puzzled. What was going on? What did Randall mean? She wasn't sure if Randall was going to say more or not. She waited. They all waited.

Then just as he began to open his mouth, there came another voice, calling from the direction of the parking lot. "Max! Sarah! Come quick!"

It was Abbie, and it sounded like something was wrong.

Chapter Two

An Accident

Max's stomach lurched. *What is it? What's happened?* she wondered. Suddenly she shivered as a large cloud covered the sun. It was spring. It was almost Easter. But oddly, the day seemed to be getting colder instead of warmer.

"Come on," Max said to Sarah. "Let's see what Abbie wants."

Abbie was in the driver's seat of her blue station wagon. She had rolled down the window.

"There's an animal that needs our help," Abbie called. "Why don't you come with me, girls?" Puffs of air came from her mouth as she breathed hard. The tall woman took off her glasses, which had fogged up in the cold. Now Max could see the concerned look in her eyes.

Grandma had come hurrying up the driveway behind them. With a nod, she agreed that the girls should go and help out.

They quickly climbed into the back seat of the car and buckled up. Behind them, in the trunk, Abbie had packed several pairs of heavy gloves, a blanket, a net and a large carrier. The carrier looked big enough to hold a cat or dog.

Max felt a shiver of excitement and worry. What kind of animal would they be rescuing? "Abbie," she began to ask, "where are we – "

"Can't talk now. Can't talk while I drive. Have to try to remember the way," Abbie replied. "Sorry." She put the car into gear and off they went.

Abbie muttered directions to herself as she drove. Max and Sarah sat quietly, not even talking to one another. They didn't want to disturb Abbie.

They headed away from the town of Maple Hill and out into the countryside. The weak sunlight vanished. Max was surprised as gentle snowflakes began to drift down over the fields and forests.

"OK, we should be getting near," said Abbie slowly. She peered ahead, her neck craning. "Can either of you see a red house nearby?"

11

Max could see a long dirt driveway. At the end of it was a red house. "Right there, Abbie," she said, pointing.

"Oh, good. That must be it," Abbie said with a sigh of relief. "Laura Flanagan called me from here. She has a dog kennel."

A kennel? Why were they going to a dog kennel? Max wondered. But Abbie was concentrating on steering around the deep potholes in the driveway. Max glanced at Sarah, but she simply shrugged with a puzzled look on her face.

Finally Abbie slowed down and pulled over beside the red house. A man with a red beard and a black jacket came hurrying over.

"Hello, hello," he called, as Abbie, Max and Sarah got out of the car.

Max could hardly hear his words. The sound of barking filled the air. High yips and low woofs came from a low building to the right. Max knew it had to be the kennel.

"I'm Abigail from Wild Paws and Claws. Are you Mr. Flanagan?" asked Abbie abruptly. She peered though the round frames of her glasses. "Where is Mrs. Flanagan?"

"I'm Clive Flanagan. It was my wife, Laura, who called you," he said. He had to raise his voice to be heard above the barking. "I'm so glad you're here. We're very worried. We've found a wild animal that we think is injured. For certain it's unconscious."

Max's heart twisted. An unconscious animal? That sounded serious. She felt sad to think of an animal hurt or in danger of dying. But over top of the sadness was a good feeling. The Flanagans wanted to help the animal. And she, Sarah and Abbie wanted to help, too. If they all did what they could, maybe everything would be all right.

"Let me take a look," Abbie replied to Mr. Flanagan.

Then Abbie turned to Max and Sarah. "Girls, please bring the carrier from the car. Lay the blanket inside first. And would you bring me a pair of gloves, please?"

The girls carried the animal crate into the house behind Mr. Flanagan and Abbie. Even with the door closed behind them, they could still hear the excited barks of the dogs. Mr. Flanagan led them down the hall and into a bright warm kitchen. A woman crouched on the floor beside an old playpen. There was mesh across the wooden bars. Several worn blankets covered the bottom of the pen. The woman looked up as they came in.

"Hello," she greeted them. "I'm Laura Flanagan.

And here is the patient. We're so sorry we weren't able to bring her to you. But several of our dogs are expecting to deliver pups any time now. We really need to be here with them."

"Of course," said Abbie quickly.

"We keep this playpen in our kitchen at all times," Mrs. Flanagan went on to explain. "We never know when we're going to need it. Sometimes we put the new pups in here. Sometimes a boarder needs to stay in the house with us for a night or two."

Bursting with curiosity, Max stepped closer. She peered into the playpen. What kind of animal was in there? But she couldn't see anything under the folds of the tattered blankets.

"Just a minute and we'll have a look," said Abbie, as she began putting on her gloves. Abbie was an expert wildlife rescuer. She knew a lot about animals, and she knew how to stay safe around them. She always wore heavy gloves when handling a wild animal.

Abbie slowly reached into the playpen. Gently she moved the top blanket to the side. As she did, she revealed first one long, large white ear and then another. Each ear had a black tip. Then Max could see a furry brownish face, a black nose and two long ears. There was a rabbit in the playpen – but it wasn't moving and its eyes were closed.

Max moaned, seeing the beautiful animal lying so still. "Is it breathing?"

"Yes, Max," Abbie said reassuringly. She pulled the blanket back even further. Now Max could see the animal's sides moving in and out. "It's breathing, but it's definitely unconscious."

"A rabbit!" exclaimed Sarah softly. She clasped her hands in delight. "A rabbit for Easter!"

"It does *look* like a rabbit, Sarah," Abbie said. "But I don't think it is. Let's have a better look."

As Abbie lifted the brown furry animal in her gentle hands, Mr. Flanagan spoke. "Laura didn't tell you much on the phone, Ms Abernathy. But we found this poor critter just outside the stand of trees in our field. We were walking with two of our dogs. Luckily, they were on leads. Otherwise . . . " Mr. Flanagan wiped his brow and shook his head.

"She didn't move," Mrs. Flanagan explained in a worried voice. "We just happened upon her, and at first we thought . . . " Mrs. Flanagan glanced at the girls, who were listening intently to her every word. "Well, at first we thought she was dead. But then Clive held the dogs back as I took a closer look. We were pretty sure she was breathing."

15

"We took the dogs home and came back right away with a pair of gloves. She was still there. She hadn't moved and was still was unconscious," Mr. Flanagan went on. "We knew she had to be in trouble."

Laura Flanagan spread her hands helplessly. "We heard about your clinic when you had your open house. So we called you right away. Can you help her?"

"I'll do whatever I can," Abbie said, and Mrs. Flanagan looked reassured.

The animal's long legs dangled limply, and Abbie gathered them up. She cradled the animal in her arms. "There, there," she murmured softly. "There, there. Let's have a better look at you."

Max leaned forward, wanting to get a better look too.

The long-eared animal had brown fur on its back and sides, and white fur on its tummy. Its front and back legs were white too. It was beautiful. Max could just imagine how soft the rabbit's fur would feel. But she shook her head slightly and reminded herself: Abbie wasn't sure it was a rabbit!

After only one glance at the animal, Abbie was certain. "Nope," she said. "This certainly isn't a rabbit."

16

Max wasn't the only one who was surprised. She saw the surprise in the faces of Sarah and Mr. and Mrs. Flanagan, too.

"This is a hare," explained Abbie. "A snowshoe hare. And she's a female. Snowshoe hares change colour in fall and spring. In the winter they're white, so they're camouflaged in the snow. In the summer, they're brown. See how our friend here is exchanging her white hair for brown hair?"

Max nodded. Even the hare's face was mostly brown with a few small white patches.

"And look." Abbie gently touched the hare's right hind foot. "See her large hind feet? They are much bigger and broader than a rabbit's. Look, they're furry on the bottom and padded with hairs. These are the 'snowshoes' that help the hare spread out its weight as it runs through deep snow."

A snowshoe hare for Easter! Max felt tingly all over. She had never seen a snowshoe hare before.

Now Abbie examined the hare's left hind leg. Max saw a red patch on it. She caught her breath.

"Hmm, there's some blood here," Abbie noted calmly.

Abbie looked at the motionless hare without speaking for a moment. Then she said to Max, "Could you please open the door of the carrier?"

Max hurried to help out, swinging the door wide as Abbie placed the hare in the carrier and carefully nestled her into the brown blanket.

"Do you think she'll be all right?" Mrs. Flanagan asked worriedly. "Is her leg very badly hurt?" She gazed earnestly into Abbie's face.

Abbie shook her head. "I don't know," she told them. Then she stood up. "But we'll do our best to help her."

"Oh, but wait," Mrs. Flanagan insisted. She put her hand on Abbie's arm. "You can't go yet. That's not all. When we went back to get the hare, Clive put the gloves on and picked her up, and we were just about to leave when . . . " Mrs. Flanagan reached into the corner of the playpen and lifted the edge of the blanket.

Again Max leaned closer to peer into the playpen. She gasped at what she saw.

Chapter Three

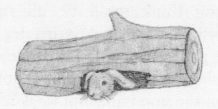

Don't Be Afraid

"A baby hare!" Max cried. Then she remembered she had to speak more softly. Wild animals were easily frightened by loud noises. "There's a baby hare here, too!" she repeated in a quieter voice.

She stared with amazement at the tiny creature crouching at the bottom of the playpen. He was like a miniature version of his mother. His little ears even had black ear-tips, like his mother's. The only differences were that his fur was completely brown, and his black eyes were wide open.

"Yes," Mrs. Flanagan said. "We just happened to see him in the bushes as we were walking away."

Max couldn't stop looking at the baby hare. He

hadn't moved a muscle. "He's so still," she marvelled. "It's as if he thinks that if he stays perfectly still, no one will notice him."

"And he's right," Abbie agreed. "That's one of the main ways that snowshoe hares protect themselves from predators." She squatted beside the playpen for a better look.

"Is he old enough to hop?" asked Sarah.

"Oh, yes," Abbie nodded. "You see, hares don't build nests like rabbits do. They just stomp down the grass under a protected area, such as a tree trunk, and give birth on the ground. Leverets — that's what baby hares are called — can see right away. And they quickly learn to hop. In fact, the day they are born, as soon as their fur is dry, they can move around."

"Wow!" Max exclaimed. She knew that puppies and kittens were born blind and helpless. She remembered that Tuffy, the baby bobcat, couldn't see or hear until she was nearly two weeks old.

"But where are the other babies? Why weren't they with this one?" Mrs. Flanagan was asking Abbie.

"Well, as soon as they can move, the babies separate — from their mother and from one another," Abbie explained. "They stay safer that way. One might hide under a log, like this one did, and another under a shrub. The mother snowshoe hare pays a visit only once a day, usually at night. All the babies come out and nurse together. Then they return to their hiding places. The mother hare must have been attacked by some kind of animal just after she finished nursing. That's the only explanation for finding her so close to her baby. Both mom and baby are lucky to be alive. It may be that the Flanagans came along with their dogs just in the nick of time and scared the attacker away."

Max smiled gratefully at Mr. and Mrs. Flanagan.

Abbie rose to her feet. "OK, if we're taking the mother hare, the baby needs to come along, too," she said firmly. "Here, Max. You do it. Put on these gloves first. And try to be as quiet as possible."

Thrilled to be trusted with the important task, Max slipped on Abbie's gloves. As she reached down toward the baby hare, it bravely remained motionless. Max gently picked it up. She used two hands, but the delicate little animal could have fit in the palm of one of her hands. She was surprised at how light he was — he weighed as little as a tennis ball!

Moving carefully, Max brought her precious bundle over to the carrier. She could feel him trembling, and she could see the sides of his belly

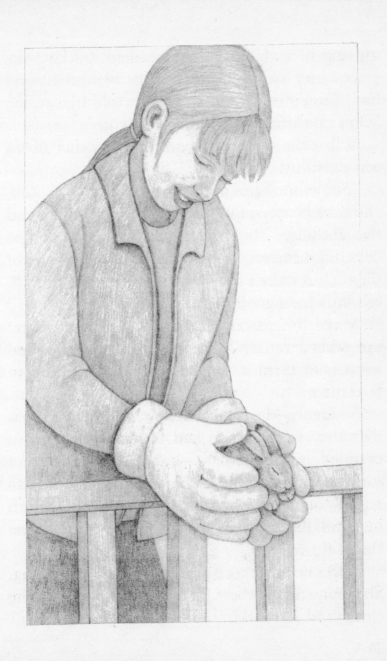

moving in and out as he breathed quickly. She placed him inside and tucked the blanket around him. "You'll be safe in here," she told him softly. "Don't be afraid. We'll look after you."

When she stood up again, Max saw that Abbie was frowning.

"Snowshoe hares in this part of the country usually have between two and five babies," Abbie said thoughtfully. "This baby looks to be about two days old. Leverets are pretty good at taking care of themselves quite early – but they need their mother's milk for a good three or four weeks."

Max felt her stomach twist. Where exactly were the other leverets? Were they alive? What would happen to them if their mother didn't return to feed them?

Suddenly Max realized how important it was that they hurry. They had to find someone to examine the mother hare – soon. They had to find someone to take care of her injuries. She had to regain consciousness and then they had to return her and her baby to where the Flanagans had found them.

Abbie seemed to be thinking the same thing. She jumped to her feet. "Now we need to get to the clinic and have this mother hare looked after."

Abbie sounded confident and optimistic that the hare would be cared for quickly, but Max wasn't fooled. She knew that Abbie was an excellent rehabilitator. She knew that Abbie was great at caring for wild animals while they healed from injuries. But Abbie had always counted on the Wild Paws and Claws volunteer vet to provide all the medical care for the animals – and the vet was retired.

Now there was no one at the clinic who could help an injured snowshoe hare. Max gulped. What if the hare remained unconscious? Or, what if she woke up, but her leg didn't heal properly? Hares depended on speed to escape from predators. If a hare couldn't move quickly it could be in severe danger. And if a mother hare with nursing babies was caught by a predator . . .

Just then Max remembered Mrs. Peach's words. After Max had told her that the clinic didn't have a vet anymore, Mrs. Peach had said, "Oh, but that can't be a problem. Not now, anyway." And then Randall had offered to help.

But what had they meant? Did Randall really have a solution to their problem? Perhaps he did.

Max needed to find out. And soon!

Chapter Four

Will She Be All Right?

"OK, girls. Please come and give us a hand."

Abbie and Mr. Flanagan carried the carrier to the back of the station wagon, and Max and Sarah opened the trunk door and cleared a place for the carrier. Abbie strapped it down securely. Then Mr. Flanagan squeezed Abbie's hands and patted Max and Sarah on their shoulders.

"Thank you so much," he said to them all.

"We'll call later and find out if the hare is going to be OK," Mrs. Flanagan added with a hopeful smile. She pulled her sweater tightly around her in the cold air.

"All right," agreed Abbie briskly. "Do you think

you can remember exactly where you found her? The exact place in the field where you found her and her baby?"

Mrs. Flanagan thought for a minute. "I think so," she said.

"Good," Abbie replied. "Because we're going to try and return soon with these two. When this mom is alert and active again, we'll want to release her and her baby just where you first saw them. We want to make sure that the mother hare finds her other little ones again quickly and easily."

"OK," Mrs. Flanagan answered. "I'll try and retrace my steps, for when you *do* come back."

Max smiled. Mrs. Flanagan's hopeful words made her feel a little better.

"Drive carefully," said Mr. Flanagan. "It's starting to snow quite hard now. I don't think I can remember so much snow around Easter."

Max hadn't noticed until now, but she realized Mr. Flanagan was right. The flakes were falling heavily from the sky. Now there was a thin layer of snow on the ground.

As Abbie started up the car and pulled away from the farmhouse, Max asked if she could use her cell phone.

"Certainly," Abbie answered, surprised. "But why?

Can't it wait until we get back to the clinic?"

Max shook her head. "No," she said firmly. "It's about the hares. There might be a chance . . . " She wasn't sure how to continue. "Well, if I can make a call, it might just help us help the hares," she finished.

"Well, then of course you must use my phone," Abbie agreed. She fumbled in her bag, with her eye on the road, then passed the phone back to Max.

Max dialled her home number. Grandma picked up the phone right away.

"Grandma, it's me, Max."

"Max! Is everything all right?" came her grandmother's concerned voice.

"Yes," replied Max. "And no. We're bringing an injured snowshoe hare back to the clinic, and she needs treatment. She has one baby with her, but there are probably more waiting for her to return. And without her to feed them . . . "

Max's voice faltered. She took a breath and forced herself to continue. "I think Mrs. Peach was starting to tell us something about a vet. She said it wasn't a problem anymore. And then Randall said that he could help. I need to know what he meant. Grandma, please call Randall. Please find out what he was going to tell us."

"Certainly," Grandma agreed. "I'll do that right away. Then I'll try to reach you at the clinic."

"Thanks, Grandma." Max felt relieved as she hung up. She knew she could always count on her grandmother.

Sarah tugged her sleeve. "What did you find out?" she asked, her brow furrowed. She twirled the end of one of her braids anxiously.

Max tried to smile. "Grandma promised to call Randall and find out how he can help us," she said, spreading her hands. "I feel so helpless. It's the only thing I can think of to do."

"Well, it's worth a try," Sarah said softly, giving her friend an admiring look. "Maybe Randall can help somehow."

Abbie continued to drive in silence. Max and Sarah sat quietly in the back seat. They were both twisted sideways so they could look over the seat at the hare and her baby in the carrier. The animals were almost completely covered by the blanket. Only their ears and faces showed.

Finally Max spoke softly. "The mother is beautiful. Her face is the colour of cinnamon."

Sarah nodded. "Kind of like the freckles on my nose," she suggested.

"Yeah," Max agreed with a smile. She thought

for a minute. "You know, I think that's what we should call her – Cinnamon."

"Me, too. It's the perfect name," Sarah exclaimed. "And what about her baby?"

The girls gazed at the tiny leveret snuggled in the folds of the blanket. Max remembered how wonderful it had felt to hold him in her hands. "He's so little," she marvelled aloud. "He seemed as light as a feather. He's like a bundle of fluff."

"How about that for a name – Fluffy?" Sarah suggested.

Max smiled. "It's just right," she agreed.

Max looked at Fluffy's brown ears with their black tips. She noticed that they turned this way and that as she spoke. "Fluffy seems to have great hearing," she said.

Abbie spoke from the front seat. "That's right," she agreed. "His ears are cup-shaped. It's the best shape for gathering sounds. Hares have an amazing sense of hearing."

"I've never seen a snowshoe hare before," Max told her.

"Me neither," Sarah chimed in. "And I've lived in Maple Hill all my life!"

"That's not unusual," Abbie told them. "Most people have seen rabbits, because they come out during the day. But hares rest in the bushes and thickets and only come out at night. And even then, they stay along the edges of the forest."

Abbie watched the road carefully as she drove. The windshield wipers were on, pushing the snow aside as it collected on the glass. "They have to look out for predators such as owls, lynx, bobcats, foxes and wolves."

Max was silent for a moment. She thought about the blood on Cinnamon's paw.

Did she dare ask?

She took a deep breath and looked at the back of Abbie's head. "Abbie, do you think Cinnamon will be OK?" Max said, her voice cracking.

Abbie didn't look back at her, but her voice softened. "I really don't know," she said.

"But what will we do? What if she stays unconscious? How can we help her without a veterinarian?" Max asked, her voice rising anxiously. "And we don't have much time. She has to get back to her other babies . . . "

Abbie didn't answer right away.

"We'll have to do our best," she said finally.

Max nodded. Neither she nor Sarah said another word, but Max didn't take her eyes off Cinnamon and Fluffy for the rest of the ride.

Chapter Five

We Need a Vet

When Max felt the car slow and turn, she faced forward. They were driving through the open gateway to Wild Paws and Claws.

Abbie parked the station wagon, unfolded her long legs from behind the driver's wheel and hurried to open the trunk. "Could you two carry Cinnamon and Fluffy in the carrier?" she asked. "I'll go ahead and unlock the clinic door."

Max and Sarah gently lifted the carrier out of the car. The blanket still covered most of the two hares. Cinnamon's big eyes were still closed. Fluffy seemed to shrink even further into the folds of the blanket.

"I want them to be OK," Sarah said anxiously, looking from the helpless furry animals to Max.

"Don't worry. I'm sure they will be," Max said.

But both girls knew that not all the animals that came to the clinic survived.

Now when Max spoke, there was a lump in her throat. "We really need a wild-animal vet. Remember that pet veterinarian we called when we found Tuffy? He couldn't help us." She swallowed hard. "No one knows as much about wild animals as a wild-animal vet!"

The wind had picked up and the air seemed a lot colder. It was mid-afternoon, but the sky was dark with clouds. As they crossed the parking lot, Max felt chilled right through her jacket. Her shoes were making footprints in the snow.

They walked slowly, careful not to jar or jerk their precious cargo. The cold wind blew again, and snow whirled around their legs. They climbed the steps to the clinic door. Earlier in the week, preparing for Easter, they had made colourful flowers from tissue paper and strung them from the clinic doorway and windows so that they dangled and blew in the spring air. Now the snowflakes danced with them.

Max helped open the unlocked door as Sarah

carefully manoeuvred the carrier inside. Abbie was just coming toward the door. "Here, I'll help you, Sarah," she offered, pushing her glasses up on her nose and reaching out for one of the carrier handles.

Max followed Abbie and Sarah down the hall. They entered one of the examination rooms and placed the carrier gently on the floor against one of the walls. Max dimmed the light.

Abbie opened the carrier door. Gently, she pulled the blanket folds aside. She looked for a while at the animals, as if she were trying to assess their condition. Then she closed the door. "I can't do much for the hares at the moment," she said worriedly, "but I do need to tend the penned animals before night comes and the snow gets any heavier. Maybe while I'm feeding the others, I'll think of someone we can ask to help us out. And if not, I'll just have to try fixing up Cinnamon's foot myself . . . somehow."

Max quickly spoke up. "We could help you," she offered. "Or do you think Sarah and I should stay here with the hares until you come back?"

"I don't think our new guests should be left alone," Abbie said thoughtfully. "Perhaps it would be better if you and Sarah kept an eye on these two. But come and get me right away if the mother seems to be coming to. All right? I'll try to be quick."

As Abbie laced up her boots, Max dialled her home phone number.

"Mom, could I please speak to Grandma?" she asked.

"Grandma isn't here right now, Max," her mother told her. "She's gone out for a while, I think."

Max's throat tightened. "Mom, I really need to speak to her. Please, please have her call me at Wild Paws when she gets back."

"All right, Max," Ms. Kearney promised. "Is everything all right?" she added, worried.

"Well, not exactly," Max replied, "but if I could speak to Grandma, it would really help. I'll explain it all to you later."

"At dinnertime," her mother said firmly.

"Yes," Max agreed and hung up the phone.

Abbie glanced at her wristwatch. It slipped and slid around her thin wrist. "It's already 4:30," Abbie reported. "I'll be back in half an hour." She saw the worried looks on the girls' faces. "Cinnamon will be fine at least until then. And who knows? When I get back I can have a look through some of the medical books that Dr. Jacobs left behind. I might find some helpful tips. And I do know some first aid. Perhaps I can patch her up myself after all," Abbie suggested valiantly, as she put on her jacket.

Max felt tears come to her eyes, but she tried not to cry. Instead she smiled bravely back at Abbie. Crying wouldn't help, but getting hold of Grandma just might.

Why wasn't Grandma calling back? What had she heard from Randall? Or maybe she hadn't even been able to get hold of him.

Chapter Six

Whitey?

"So, how about we take turns waiting with Cinnamon and Fluffy in the clinic?" Max suggested. "One of us can watch over them while the other one of us works in the office. That way at least we'll get some things done."

"Good idea," said Sarah with a smile.

"Would you like the first turn with them?" asked Max.

Sarah nodded quickly.

"OK, you stay here, then, and I'll head to the office," Max said.

Sarah headed back inside the examination room. Max put her jacket on and walked through the snow to the small office building. When she got inside, she headed to Abbie's office at the back. Even though it was not even five o'clock, it seemed dark and gloomy inside. She had to turn on all the lights.

Max glanced at Abbie's overflowing bookshelves and her couch stacked with mounds of wildlife magazines and file folders. There was lots of tidying up to be done. She grinned at the thought. She knew that this was a never-ending job. Abbie never put anything away. Maybe when it was Sarah's turn in the office she could have a go at it!

Hmm . . . There were always many letters to be written, too. Max remembered that a child who had visited Wild Paws last month had written to them. The little girl had really liked Tippy the red fox, and she wanted to know more about wild foxes, such as what they eat and where they live.

I think I'll write to her with some information, Max thought.

Max went to the bookshelves and picked out a handful of wildlife books. She knew she could find lots of helpful facts in them, if only she could stop worrying about Cinnamon. Max tried to think about the girl's questions. She tried to get some real work done.

But every few minutes Max looked up at the

clock. She wanted it to be her turn to be at the clinic. She wanted it to be her turn to watch Cinnamon and Fluffy.

Finally Max sighed. It was impossible. She was too worried about Cinnamon and Fluffy and the other leverets. No matter how hard she tried, she just couldn't stop thinking about the snowshoe hares.

There was no way Max could think about foxes right now, much as she loved them. She would respond to the girl's letter tomorrow.

She looked up "snowshoe hare" in Abbie's biggest and best animal book and found an informative page with colour photos of hares. One photo showed a hare sitting under a bush on a snowy winter day. It looked just like Cinnamon, except that it didn't have any cinnamon colour on it at all! It was white with black-tipped ears.

Maybe Cinnamon needs two names, Max thought with a grin. Cinnamon for the summer, and Whitey for the winter!

The caption under the photo read, *The winter food of snowshoe hares includes the bark, twigs and buds of woody plants, such as maple trees and willow trees. They also eat the needles of most kinds of conifer trees. In the summer, hares eat plants such as clover, green grasses, dandelions, strawberries and daisies.*

Another photo showed a hare leaping across the snow. The caption under that photo read, *The hare can run faster than most pursuers. It races across the trails or 'runways' that it has made in the snow. A hare will look after its trails, snipping away any twigs along the path that might slow it down when it is being chased.*

Max shivered to think of Cinnamon being caught by a predator. Is that how she'd been knocked unconscious? Was that how her leg had been hurt? I guess we'll never know, she thought. But at least she's safe here with us.

Just then, the door to the office opened. Sarah came in with a flurry of snow.

"Whew," she said, brushing off her jacket. "It's really getting white out there!"

"How are Cinnamon and Fluffy?" asked Max. She jumped up to get her jacket and shoes on.

Sarah lifted her shoulders. "Well, Fluffy's OK. But Cinnamon . . . " She frowned. "I really don't know. She's still unconscious. And I can't see her leg, so it's hard to know if she's still bleeding."

Max was just putting on her jacket, anxious to go and see the hares, when the phone rang. She went to answer it right away. At Wild Paws and Claws, every call could be an important one. Every call could be someone needing help for an injured wild animal.

Or maybe – her heart beat faster – it was Grandma with some good news.

"Hello?" Max answered.

"Hello. This is Mrs. Flanagan calling. I just want to ask how the bunnies are managing so far."

Max smiled. It hadn't been long since they had left the Flanagan farm. But she knew how Mrs. Flanagan felt. When you're worried about an injured animal, a short time can seem like forever.

"She seems just the same. No better and no worse," Max answered honestly. It was the most reassuring thing she could think of to say.

"Well, I guess that's good," Mrs. Flanagan said. "I also wanted to tell you that I've remembered exactly where I found the hare and the baby. I'm so worried about those little leverets. Especially as it seems to be snowing a lot, and getting quite cold and windy. It would be wonderful if you could treat the mother hare and then come right back out here early tomorrow morning."

"Yes," agreed Max. "I hope we can do that."

"Well, perhaps we'll see you bright and early then," Mrs. Flanagan ended. "Goodbye, Max."

"Bye," Max replied, and as she hung up the phone, the lights flickered. Off-on-off-on.

Then the office was plunged into darkness.

Chapter Seven

Storm!

"Oh, no," moaned Sarah. "This is spooky."

Max gulped. It *was* kind of spooky with all the lights out. "I guess the wind must have knocked down a power line."

"Now what do we do?" Sarah said nervously.

"Well," Max said, "we still have to look after the hares. Let's both go over to the clinic and stay with them. Abbie will be back any minute."

Max picked up her jacket, and she and Sarah headed to the front door. But all of a sudden, the girls jumped. There was a loud pounding at the door, and then it flew open. Someone burst inside.

But who was it? They couldn't tell at first in the dimming light.

Then he took off his hat and turned his face to them. Max sucked in her breath. It was Randall!

"Randall!" she cried. "What are you doing here?"

"What am I doing here?" he answered. "I thought you needed help! That's what your grandmother told me. That's what *you* told me when I was here earlier."

He shook the snow off his hat and the arms of his jacket, and ran his fingers through his damp hair.

Max frowned. "Well, we do need help. Or, I mean, Cinnamon, the snowshoe hare, needs help. Did Grandma tell you? She's unconscious and bleeding." She paused and looked at the young man. "But what can you do?"

For a moment, Randall didn't answer. Max and Sarah just stared at him.

Then finally, he spoke. "I'm going to be a veterinarian. That is, I'm studying to be a vet, a wild-animal vet . . . "

Max's eyes widened.

"Oh, that's excellent!" Sarah cried.

Max felt the first stirrings of hope. She thought

of the mother snowshoe hare and her beautiful brown fur. She imagined Cinnamon bounding through a snowy meadow, graceful and free, or zigzagging away from a swooping great horned owl to safety in the forest. She thought of Fluffy and his brothers and sisters growing up healthy and strong. Maybe tomorrow she would get to see the others.

But then Max bit her lip. She pictured the hare's still body. She pictured the blood she had seen on Cinnamon's leg. Could Randall really help Cinnamon?

Max looked at Randall doubtfully. "Abbie's been working with animals for years, and she isn't sure she can help Cinnamon," she told him.

Randall looked back at her. "I can try," he repeated. "I had hands-on experience this last year at university. We learned how to stitch and treat animals. I took a special seminar that focused on wild animals."

Max nodded once, then again. A smile spread across her face. "So let's get over to the clinic," she said quickly. "That's where the hares are. Let's go right away."

"OK," Randall agreed. "But it's snowing quite hard. Maybe you two should stay here, and I'll go alone."

Max and Sarah stared at the young man.

"Are you joking?" Sarah laughed.

"There's no way that a little snow would stop us from coming with you!" Max added cheerfully.

Randall shook his head. "You girls are obviously as animal crazy as I am," he said.

"Maybe even more!" said Max as she pulled on her jacket. "OK, let's go!"

Chapter Eight

Making a Mistake

Max and Sarah were all ready to go as Randall put his hat back on. Then Max opened the office door and led the way toward the clinic.

The wind was very strong. Snow was whirling and swirling.

"It's no wonder the power is out," Sarah commented, grabbing at her hat as it almost blew away.

The three walked quickly across the yard. Eagerly, Max opened the door to the clinic and she, Randall and Sarah hurried inside. Sarah closed the door quickly behind her.

Max tried the light switch, but nothing happened.

"We need some flashlights or candles," Randall said.

"I'll go and get Abbie," Sarah suggested.

But Max put her hand on Sarah's arm. "No, it's OK," she responded, thinking hard. Abbie must still be busy with the animals. "I think I know what to do." A pleased smile crossed Max's face. She snapped her fingers. The emergency supply kit! Abbie took one with her when she went to rescue animals, and she left one in the clinic, too. Abbie had shown her where it was kept.

Max made her way down the dark hallway, feeling her way along the wall. "Here it is," she announced. She opened the kit and felt through it. As soon as she found one of the flashlights, she flicked it on. The warm beam played across Randall's and Sarah's relieved faces.

"Great," cheered Sarah. "Now let's check on Cinnamon."

Max handed Sarah the other flashlight, and Sarah led the way to the examination room. The two girls hurried to the carrier. Max peered inside. There were Cinnamon and Fluffy, both still wrapped in the blanket. Max saw Fluffy's nose twitch as the girls bent over the box. He lifted his ears and turned them, the black tops quivering. The

baby hare's black eyes seemed to look directly into Max's.

There was a quiet moment while Max gazed back at him.

She turned to Randall. "Will you take a peek at Cinnamon's leg now?"

Randall hesitated.

"Randall?" Max said. "Will you take a look at Cinnamon's leg?"

But Randall still didn't respond.

Max and Sarah looked at each other, puzzled.

"Randall, is something wrong?" Max asked, gently.

Randall swallowed. He nodded once. Finally he spoke. "I'm worried," he admitted. "I thought I could do this . . . but maybe it's best for Cinnamon if I don't try."

Max stared at Randall. "What do you mean?" she asked. "How can you say that?"

"I love animals. I always have." Randall's voice sounded strained and his face was glum. He stepped closer to the carrier. He still hadn't taken his eyes off Cinnamon and Fluffy.

He gulped and went on. "I was doing a practice month at a veterinary clinic last month. I was looking after a young injured squirrel. I made a mistake and . . . well, the squirrel died." Randall stopped speaking and cleared his throat.

"Oh, Randall, that's really sad," Max said.

"Yes, it is," echoed Sarah.

"I made a big mistake," Randall said. "And what if I make another one now . . . with Cinnamon?" He bit his lip and folded his arms.

"But Randall," said Max, "it was a mistake, right?"

"Everyone makes mistakes," offered Sarah.

"True. But when you make a mistake and an animal dies . . . "

Max, Sarah and Randall stood in silence for a few moments.

Max looked out the window. In the fading light she could see the snow thickly falling.

They were alone. And Cinnamon was hurt. And Fluffy and his siblings needed her to live.

"Randall, it must feel awful, but won't it feel worse if Cinnamon dies, too, because you wouldn't look at her?" asked Max. "And Fluffy? And Cinnamon's other babies? If you could help her to get better, we could return her to her babies and they all might survive."

Randall didn't answer.

Sarah looked at Max and shrugged. Her eyes were watery.

Max sighed. She almost felt like crying too.

But then Randall finally spoke. "You're right," he said softly. And with a determined look on his face, he slipped on some examining gloves and reached into the carrier. "Light, please, Max," he said.

Quickly, Max shifted the beam of the flashlight so that Randall could see what he was doing. Gently he lifted the unconscious hare out of the blanket. Holding Cinnamon firmly in his arms, he stroked her fur.

Max shone the light on the hare as Randall turned her slightly this way and then that. He examined her face, her stomach and then her leg.

"What do you think?" Max asked finally. "Is she going to be all right?"

"Well, she has been unconscious for a long time. Until she comes around, it's hard to know if this might be the sign of a head wound – or how serious it might be. But the good news is that her leg wound doesn't look too serious. It needs some cleaning up, but it isn't too deep to fix," Randall replied. He looked up at Max and said, "You know, I think I can do it. I think I can help heal her leg."

And just as Randall finished speaking, Cinnamon seemed to stir in his arms. Her ears moved, and her legs twitched, and she was pulling them up tight against her body.

"She's waking up!" Randall cried in relief. Quickly he got a better grip on the animal, holding her more firmly. "She may take a while to become fully conscious, but this is very good. Very good," he repeated, nodding happily.

Max felt a burst of happiness. Cinnamon's leg would be all right – and soon she would be awake.

"OK," Randall said. "As she comes around, she may be very frightened and panicky. It would be better if you girls left the room." His voice was professional and polite. "But please set the flashlight down here so I can see to put her back in the carrier."

Max and Sarah immediately did what the student vet asked. Then they hurried out into the hallway.

"Oh, Sarah, isn't it great?" Max cried. She rushed to hug her friend.

"Yes!" Sarah agreed. "Absolutely, fabulously, marvellously wonderful!"

Before the girls had a chance to talk more, they heard the clinic door opening.

"Max? Sarah?" It was Abbie. "Can you give me a hand?"

"We're right here!" Max called out. The two girls hurried down the hallway to greet Abbie. They could see the beam of her flashlight dancing on the walls. The clinic's front door was slamming open and shut in the wind, and snow was blowing everywhere.

"Sorry I took so long," Abbie told them. She held a large flashlight in one hand and a large bag in her arms, and she was trying to push the door shut. "I fed the animals, and when I got back to the office, I realized that the power had gone out. It took me some time to find the emergency flashlight." Abbie paused. "I hope you weren't nervous," she said.

"No," Max began. "We weren't. Actually . . . "

Abbie nodded. "I didn't think you would be. And how's Cinnamon? Is she all right?"

Max grinned and nodded. "Oh, yes. She's fine! Abbie, guess what?"

But Abbie was distracted. With a final shove, she closed the door with a bang. "There we go. Now, here, Max. Can you take this bag? Sarah, can you take this flashlight?"

The girls quickly did as she asked.

As Abbie bent to take off her wet shoes, Max opened her mouth to tell Abbie the exciting news about Cinnamon. But she still didn't get a chance.

Abbie lifted her chin and peered up at the girls through her damp glasses. "Guess what?" she asked. She had a big smile on her face. "I had a wonderful idea!"

Chapter Nine

Easter Adventure!

"I think we should have a slumber party here in the clinic tonight!" Abbie suggested. She stood up and took off her glasses. She wiped them briskly on her sleeve, and then put them back on again. "I know it's a Sunday and tomorrow is a school day. But it might not be a good idea to head home in this weather. And, most importantly, if we all stay, we can keep watch on the hares overnight. What do you think? If I can patch Cinnamon's leg up and she's improved, we can zip out at the crack of dawn and return her and her baby to the rest of their family. Then I can drop you off at school before the bell rings."

"Oh, wow," Max breathed. "That sounds great!"

Sarah quickly agreed. "Yes, I'd love to," she said.

"Terrific," Abbie said. "That bag you're holding, Max, has some special treats in it. We'll need something to munch on for dinner, so I brought some things from the office storeroom and my mini-fridge – cheese and crackers, cocoa powder and milk for making chocolate drinks. I even have some bread and jam and a few bananas. Now, I'll just go and take a peek at Cinnamon while you two make a quick call to your parents to make sure it's OK. Here. You can use my cell phone."

As Sarah began punching in her phone number, Abbie looked at Max. "Even if Cinnamon were fine now, it would be too dark to return her to the field. We'd never find the babies at night and in this snow."

Max put her hand on Abbie's arm. "Abbie – " she said.

"Those babies can't be without their mother for too long," Abbie continued. She had a worried look on her face.

Max nodded. "But Abbie – "

"Then again, if Cinnamon's injured . . . " Abbie pressed her lips together. "Well, we'll just have to hope for the best, won't we? I'll take a close look at her now and then I'll try going through some of Dr. Jacobs' medical books, like I mentioned. Maybe I could even try to reach him on the phone and get some long-distance advice," she said, crossing her arms and frowning. "I'm sure there's something I can do to help Cinnamon's leg heal."

Sarah was off the phone. "Can you stay?" Abbie asked her.

"Yes," Sarah said. "But Abbie, listen! Please listen to what Max is trying to tell you!"

Max put her hand on Abbie's arm. "I have good news!" she said.

Abbie took off her glasses one more time. Once more she wiped them and put them back on. Now she looked at Max directly. "Well, tell me," she said. "What is it?"

"Remember I called Grandma from the car earlier? Well, her friend's nephew, Randall, is studying to be a wild-animal vet. He's here now, and he's taken a look at Cinnamon. He says her wound will be fine. He can treat her! And while he was examining her, she started to come to!"

"That's wonderful! Oh, that's wonderful," Abbie said with relief. Then she peered over her glasses at Max sternly. "Why didn't you say so before now?" she demanded, and then quickly gave Max an exaggerated wink to show that she was teasing.

Without drawing another breath, Abbie resumed

her busy plans. "Where is Randall? In with Cinnamon? Then I'll just pop in and double-check that everything is all right. We'll fix her up, get some shut-eye, and then, first thing in the morning, we'll get her back to her babies, right? Sleeping bag, blankets, pillows . . . You girls know where I keep those things. Would you get them from the office, please? Take this flashlight if you need it. Oh, and I'll take that bag back from you, Max. I'll put it in the storeroom. I think that's where we'll hole up for the night."

Abbie took the bag from Max, tossed off her jacket and strode briskly down the hallway. As Max phoned her parents, she watched Abbie duck into the storeroom doorway, set down the bag and then hurry toward the wounded hare and her baby. Max spoke to her mother, who told her that she could certainly spend the night at the clinic. After she said goodnight, Max could hear Abbie introducing herself to Randall.

"Whooo are you, young man? Are you Randall? Good job. I'll be your assistant. Let's take care of Cinnamon immediately."

Then the two girls hurried out the door into the snowy evening.

Outside, Max grinned at her friend. "A sleepover! We're going to stay all night with Cinnamon and Fluffy – and then help return them to the wild!"

Sarah grinned back. "I can't believe it," she said excitedly.

The girls loaded up with a sleeping bag, blankets and pillows. They even found an air mattress. Then they quickly made their way back to the clinic and began organizing the supplies.

By the time Randall and Abbie reappeared, Max and Sarah had arranged a cozy eating and sleeping area in the empty storeroom. They had cut slices of cheese and arranged crackers on a plate. They had even found blank paper, scissors and markers and had happily sat cross-legged, making cutouts of Easter hares to decorate the plate!

"How is she? How's Cinnamon?" Max asked Randall as he appeared in the doorway.

"She's fine," he said. He grinned in amazement. "She's just fine. She doesn't seem to have any side effects from being unconscious. No head injury. Her leg needed a few stitches, but I was able to put them all in."

"That's terrific!" Max cried. "Good work, Randall!"

"We knew you could do it," Sarah chimed in.

Randall smiled sheepishly and ran his fingers through his tangled hair.

Abbie slapped her hand on Randall's shoulder. "This fine fellow has done a great job. I agree with him that we can certainly release Cinnamon and Fluffy back into the wild tomorrow morning!" Then Abbie's smiled faded a little. "I hope Mrs. Flanagan remembers where she found these two hares," she remarked thoughtfully.

"Oh, Abbie!" Max cried. "Mrs. Flanagan phoned while you were out. She *does* remember where they were. So we won't have any trouble in the morning!"

Abbie's face beamed. "Well, that's good. That's very good indeed," she said.

Max was thrilled. What an Easter adventure this had turned into!

The girls persuaded Randall to stay and eat with them. Everyone snacked on cheese and crackers and drank cold cocoa in good spirits. Afterwards, Abbie told stories about the wild animals that she had helped over the years at Wild Paws and Claws. The girls even convinced Randall to tell them a little bit about veterinary school.

Then Randall went and had one last look at Cinnamon and Fluffy. "They're both doing fine," he reported. "You might want to have a peek at them during the night, just to make sure Cinnamon isn't scratching at her stitches."

"What if she is?" Max asked quickly.

"Well, give me a call and I'll come and replace them right away," Randall said calmly. "But I'm sure she'll be fine. I gave her a little something to help her relax while I put the stitches in, so she wouldn't be bothered by them tonight. And by morning, they won't itch anymore, and she'll be alert and ready to head back home to her other young ones."

Max nodded, reassured by the young man's confident words. "Thanks, Randall," she said gratefully.

"Yes, thank you, Randall," Abbie said. She shook Randall's hand. "Perhaps we'll need you to help again sometime. Maybe this summer?"

Max held her breath.

Randall blushed. "Maybe," he said with a grin.

After taking a last good-night peek at Cinnamon and Fluffy, Max and Sarah curled up in some blankets in a corner of the supply room. Abbie chose their other offering, her sleeping bag on the air mattress. Even though her long legs dangled over the sides, she assured them that she was absolutely comfortable. Max could hardly keep her eyes open after the busy day. As soon as the flashlights were turned off, she fell right to sleep.

Chapter Ten

Safely Home

Max woke early the next morning, but not earlier than Abbie. She was just coming noisily back into the supply room. "Cinnamon looks as good as new," she told Max, as if she knew what her first question would be. "And Fluffy is just fine as well. The power is back on and the snow has already started to melt. How about some breakfast?"

Sarah opened her eyes. "What time is it?" she inquired sleepily.

"It's just after dawn. Early, yes. But we have to get to those little leverets quickly," Abbie said firmly. Then she paused. She held up a basket. "We still have some bananas, bread and jam left over from last night. Do you girls want some breakfast before we go?"

"It looks great. Thanks, Abbie," Max said politely. "But . . . I think you're right. We should take Cinnamon and Fluffy back to where the Flanagans found them as soon as possible. Cinnamon's other babies need her. They've only missed one feeding — last night's. But we don't want them to wait any longer for another feeding, do we?"

Abbie smiled. "What are we waiting for, then?" she said, clapping her hands. "OK! Sarah, please go and make sure Cinnamon and little Fluffy are comfortable in their carrier. Max, you call and let the Flanagans know that we'll be on our way soon," Abbie instructed. "I'll go and prepare the car."

Both girls bustled to do what they were asked.

In less than one hour, Max, Sarah and Abbie were back at the Flanagan farm. The road was still snowy, but the sun was shining and the warmer temperatures had returned. As they pulled up to the farmhouse, Max saw Mr. and Mrs. Flanagan ready and waiting for them.

Max and Sarah eagerly volunteered to bring the carrier containing Cinnamon and Fluffy. They followed Mr. and Mrs. Flanagan across the field. They stopped just at the edge of a stand of trees.

"This is it. This is where our dogs first spotted the mother hare. I'm certain," Mrs. Flanagan said confidently.

Max and Sarah set down the carrier.

For a moment, no one moved.

"Over there," Mrs. Flanagan said, pointing to a fallen log at the edge of the stand of trees. "That's where we found them."

Then Abbie said, "Why don't you release the hares, girls?"

Max and Sarah nodded their heads. Together they picked up the carrier and walked toward the trees. When they reached the log, they gently set the carrier down.

For a moment, they both gazed at the hares. Max could see Cinnamon's beautiful body, crouched and ready to leap into freedom. Max smiled to see her long ears twitching and turning to hear the sounds of her home. It was a joy to see Cinnamon's enormous black eyes. They were wild eyes, eyes that might never see a human again, eyes that should only be gazing at downy leverets, shoots of new grass and colourful spring blossoms.

Max knew it was best not to speak aloud. Goodbye, Cinnamon, she said in her heart.

Together, Sarah and Max reached down and

opened the door to the carrier. Max saw Cinnamon hesitate for a brief moment, and then with a scrabble and a leap and another leap, she was out of the carrier and gone.

They stood for a few moments and waited, watching Fluffy, but the leveret did not seem in a hurry to leave.

Out you go, Max urged the baby silently, but Fluffy didn't budge.

Finally Max turned and looked toward Abbie. The tall woman gestured that Max should lift the baby hare out of the carrier.

With gloved hands, Max reached into the carrier and picked up the feather-light baby hare. Her heart felt full of happiness. The little creature's eyes were shining. His nose was twitching, and his ears were turning. Maybe he remembered the smells and sounds of this forest! He seemed to know that something wonderful was about to happen!

Max stroked Fluffy soothingly with her fingertip as she walked with him toward the log. He was tiny, but he wouldn't be tiny forever. His mother was healthy and free. She would feed him tonight and the next night. She would feed his brothers and sisters, too. All the baby hares would have a chance at surviving in the wilderness, thanks to

Wild Paws and Claws – and especially Randall.

Carefully, she set the little animal underneath the log, finding a dry spot that the snow had not reached. She took one last good look at him. Goodbye, Fluffy, Max thought with a surge of joy. You're free again!

Fluffy tucked himself in, making himself as little as possible, just as a wild baby hare should.

Max turned. She and Sarah lifted the carrier and joined the others. Together they walked back toward the Flanagans' farm. Max enjoyed the sun's early-morning warmth on her face. The signs of last night's snowfall were already melting away from the fields. Birds were chirping, excited about the promise of spring. Max could once again see new green shoots poking their way up through the white.

Max knew that Cinnamon would be feeding on these tender plants. She knew that Fluffy and his siblings would be basking in the warm rays of today's spring sunshine. She knew that many other wild baby animals would soon be born.

Max gave a happy sigh of pleasure.

Yes, spring was her favourite time of the year. Definitely.

Snowshoe Hare
Information Sheet

🐾 Snowshoe hares are found throughout most of Canada and in parts of the northern United States.

🐾 A female hare is called a doe; a male hare is called a buck. Baby hares are called leverets.

🐾 The rear legs of a snowshoe hare are longer than the front legs. Picture a racecar – low in front and high in back!

🐾 Snowshoe hares stay in a home range of between 1.5 and 5 hectares. That's the size of between three and ten football fields. (The better the food supply, the smaller the home range.) Although snowshoe hares do spend most of their time alone, they sometimes run into one another as the ranges of snowshoe hares often overlap.

🐾 Snowshoe hares create runways, or paths, in their territory. The runways lead from open areas to safer cover. Hares use these runways as escape routes when they are being chased by a predator. They are also good swimmers and will take to the water if they are in danger!

❧ The snowshoe hare's white winter coat insulates 27% more than the brown summer coat.

❧ Female hares can have up to four litters in one season, depending on the environmental conditions. Although they can give birth to as many as eight leverets, the average litter size is usually two to four young.

❧ Snowshoe hares are active when there is little light: at dusk, during the night, at dawn – and on cloudy days! During the day, they nap and groom themselves.

❧ Light also tells the hare when it's time to change its coat or "moult." As the days grow shorter, the hare gradually loses its summer coat and gets its white winter coat; as the days grow longer, the hare loses its winter coat and gets its rusty-brown summer coat. Moulting takes from 70 to 75 days. The varying colour helps camouflage the snowshoe hare.